Disclaimer

This is a work of fiction. Any names, businesses, characters, events, incidents and places are either the product of the author's imagination or used in a fictitious manner. Any resemblance to actual people, living or dead, or actual events or occurrences is purely coincidental.

Our Secret

By Alessandra Bancroft
Copyright © 2015

Table of Contents

Chapter 1: Taking the Stage 4

Chapter 2: Opportunity 6

Chapter 3: Meeting Tim 8

Chapter 4: Thrown Under the Bus 13

Chapter 5: Super Bowl Sunday 16

Chapter 6: Last Chance 19

Chapter 7: Feeling Empty 24

Chapter 8: A Picture is Worth 1,000 Words 26

Chapter 9: The End 27

Chapter 10: An Act of Kindness 29

Chapter 11: Another Opportunity 31

Chapter 12: Last Chance 32

Chapter 13: Our Secret 34

My Other Books and Audio Books 37

Chapter 1: Taking the Stage

"Ahh…" Melanie breathed out in relief as she sprawled out on the new hammock she had just purchased for her large backyard. After working 10-hour days, for seven days straight training to be an assistant manager at Save 'n Bag, the grocery store she worked for, she figured a comfy hammock would be the perfect reward for all her hard work.

The hot afternoon sun beat down hard on her, causing some sweat to form on her skin. Pushing her long, dark brown hair of out of her face, she undid the top few buttons of her new work shirt, which was a little too small for her, exposing a couple of inches of her voluptuous chest. A few more buttons and her goods might have busted right out. She was just thinking about how nice it would be to live at the beach when her phone rings, jerking her out of her serenity. Fishing her phone out of her pocket, she smiled when she saw it was her boss, Paulina.

"Hey Paulina!" she said into the phone, undoing another button of her shirt. *Ahh, it felt good to breathe.* It was normal for Melanie to talk so casually with her boss. They had a good relationship. "I don't know how you manage to keep such a nice tan. You work 10 more hours a week than me! I'm out in my backyard now lying out in the sun, trying to catch up with you!"

"Melanie," Paulina said in a serious voice.

Melanie sat up and frowned, instantly sensing that something was wrong. "What's up? Everything okay?"

"I really hurt my back today," Paulina explained. "I was loading cases of coffee creamer onto the top shelf of the cooler and one of the boxes burst open on me causing me to slip and fall. I think I really threw myself out of commission."

"Oh no, that's terrible!" Melanie frowned. "Are you going to go get it checked out?"

"No, I think if I take it easy for a few days, I'll be alright. That's why I'm calling. I know you're only halfway into your training, but I'm going to ask you to do what I usually do in the mornings – set up our produce display – while I set up some easier displays. Do you think you're up to it?"

Training to be an assistant manager was intense. Save 'n Bag was a highly regarded grocery store – the company provided excellent service and products to their customers, but they expected a great deal from their employees. All managers had to oversee at least three sectors of perishable items in their stores, and every display had to look picture perfect by certain times throughout the day.

If those demands weren't met, it wasn't good for the manager in charge. It was hard yet rewarding work, and although sometimes Melanie felt discouraged, she always had Paulina to remind her how well she was doing and how her hard work might eventually lead her to moving up within the company.

Melanie scratched her head and twisted her lips in contemplation. "I don't know," she said. "Do *you* think I'm ready?"

"I think you can handle it," Paulina said. "You're my best worker. I can always count on you. Remember, you can do anything you set your mind to."

Paulina's encouraging words always made Melanie feel like she was on top of a mountain from which nobody could tear her down. "Alright," Melanie smiled. "I'll do it! I'll see you tomorrow at 8 a.m."

"Make sure you get enough rest," Paulina said. "Our new district manager will be there tomorrow. You'll want to make a good impression."

Chapter 2: Opportunity

8 a.m. came and went quickly. Melanie worked hard that morning to create the most spectacular produce display Save 'n Bag had ever seen. By the time she was done, it was almost time to open, but the other two displays that she was in charge of weren't even near finished. If the district manager walked through the door now she was done for. Just as she was rushing to get all of the trash off of the floor she heard a painful scream from a few aisles over.

Running to the commotion, she stopped in her tracks when she saw Paulina holding her back on the floor with a grimace on her face in the middle of the home goods display.,

"Are you alright?" Melanie called out. Thinking quickly, she slid open the door to one of the sliding freezers nearby and grabbed a bag of frozen vegetables. Bringing it to Paulina, she knelt down to the floor and gently pressed it against her lower back.

"Thank you Mel," Paulina managed to say. "I really thought I'd be okay doing this alone," she motioned to her display, "but I think this is more than just a sprain. I'm going to have to get this looked at by a doctor. That means I may have to go out on disability for a while."

A look of disappointment mingled with hope streaked across Melanie's face. "Do you think they would let me run your –"

Her sentence was suddenly cut off by the sound of high heels rapidly clicking on the hard floor beneath them. Before she knew it, Melanie was face to face with the woman who was the new "big boss." Melanie's first impression was that she was young and pretty. She couldn't have been much older than a college graduate, not unlike Melanie. She wore shiny black shoes, a sleek business suit and she wore her straight blond hair back with two barrettes.

"What's going on here?" she asked without so much as an introduction. Melanie could detect a slight French accent in her voice.

Dropping the bag of vegetables to the floor, Melanie quickly scrambled to get up and stuck her hand out. "Hello," she stammered. "I'm Melanie. I'm training to be an assistant manager."

The big boss took her hand and squeezed it tightly. "I'm Raylayna the district manger." Shifting her eyes down to Paulina, she said, "And you must be Paulina, the store manager," she said in a disapproving tone.

"I'd shake your hand but I think I just ripped my back out of my frame," Paulina said lightly, squeezing one eye shut in pain.

Raylayna didn't even crack a smile. "Well if you're going to need to go see a doctor then I suggest you get up off the floor and go head out now," she said before walking away to go inspect Melanie's produce display.

Melanie and Paulina exchanged bewildered looks.

"Well, she seemed like a total bitch," Paulina said matter-of-factly. "Agreed!" said Melanie as she helped Paulina to her feet and out to her car.

Chapter 3: Meeting Tim

The rest of the day was hectic and Raylayna being there made it even more nerve wracking. A few hours later, Melanie opened the office door and moved towards the wall to read her schedule for the rest of the week. As she walked inside, she noticed Raylayna sitting at the computer, speaking to someone on her cell phone.

"Well, you are officially part of store 27 now," she said to whoever she was speaking too. "You start tomorrow at 8 a.m." After hanging up, she turned to Melanie. "Hey Melanie, how are things going for you today?"

Melanie shrugged. "Pretty good except for the fact that Paulina got hurt this morning." She paused. "You know, she's been training me for a while now and I think I might have what it takes to run the store while she's out."

"I appreciate the initiative, but I think it's still too soon, seeing that you've only undergone the assistant manager training. I was just speaking to Tim, a store management trainee at the Save 'n Bag a few towns over. He is going to come here and help out for a bit. I'm sure you'll learn a lot from him. You'll meet him tomorrow at 8 a.m."

"Awesome," Melanie tried to say enthusiastically, even though her face fell. Walking into the adjacent break room, she punched out on her break and headed home. When she arrived she let her body fall into her chair. Crossing her arms, she thought to herself:

"Great. I've been working so hard to get another promotion and I just missed my chance. My boss and mentor just went out on an injury for God knows how long and now I'm stuck with this new district manager who seems like she's on a total power trip and is already starting to bring in new people. Ugggh. It's ok though. This is my store. I'll show them, who the best manager really should be!"

It took Melanie a while to fall asleep that night and when she finally did get some sleep it was filled with vivid dreams about her work place. When she woke up the next day was tired and nervous. She had some scrambled eggs and then did her best to look great for her next day. She made long curls with her beautiful brown hair that her past boyfriends had loved. She did her makeup extra nice and was sure to wear her favorite tight fitting blue shirt with her form fitting black professional trousers.

It was the first shift that she was running by herself. Standing in front of the dairy freezer doors, she held the store's inventory ordering device in her hand and stared at it blankly. *Come on Melanie,* she said in her head. *You and Paulina did this hundreds of times together.* Sticking out her tongue, she started to type in some numbers when her heart suddenly jumped out of her chest. It was the store's doorbell. It had to be that guy Tim.

Melanie made her way to the front of the store, anticipation flowing through her body. She wondered what he looked like. She wondered how he spoke. She wondered if he was nice. Most importantly, she wondered if he was any *good*.

As she neared the entrance, she could see him standing outside. Pulling open the door, she bit her tongue to stop her mouth from dropping open, but she was pretty sure she felt her eyes widen. Before her stood a tall, handsome man with dirty blonde hair and soft, sexy eyes framed by a pair of designer eyeglasses. His arms were muscular and his body was built yet slim. Although he wore a Save 'n Bag uniform, anyone could tell that his body underneath was ripped.

Melanie had never seen such a handsome man in her life, especially not at work. All morning, she thought about how she would introduce herself to him, but in the heat of the moment, all she could manage was, "What do you know about doing a milk order?"

"Oh my god, Melanie, that's all you could come up with!?" she thought furiously.

Tim smiled at her, amused. He pressed his lips together to hold back a laugh. "And they left you in charge of this place?" he teased. "No wonder they called me up in desperation."

Melanie crossed her arms over her chest her face flushing red. "It's my first shift by myself," she shot back, immediately regretting let him get such a strong reaction from her.

Tim smiled then said "I can tell you've been standing in front of the fridge."

"How do you know?" asked Melanie

Tim pointed to her chest. "Because your headlights are on."

Looking down, Melanie noticed that the cold air from the fridge went straight through her already too-tight manager shirt and had caused her nipples to stand straight up. Gasping at his audacity, she quickly folder her arms over her chest and scowled at him. She couldn't help but notice, however, at how cute his dimples where when he was smiling.

"This way" Tim said as he headed back to the dairy section with Melanie and quickly walked her through the order process. Melanie wished she could melt into the floor. They had only known each other for two minutes and already she was embarrassing herself. She had done this process plenty of times before... she couldn't believe today of all days she couldn't remember. "I bet it's because of those dreams I was having last night," she thought.

"Hey," Tim said, pulling her out of her reverie. He was frowning and pulling one of the refrigerator doors open. He reached down and grabbed a half-gallon of milk off of one of the shelves, rotating it in his hands to show her the expiration date. "This milk is dated for three days from now. It should have been marked down."

Melanie felt the red sting on her face again. "I told you, it's only my first shift."

Tim smiled again, only this time a bit friendlier. "It's okay, I won't tell Raylayna." He put the milk back on the shelf and winked at her. "It'll be our secret."

Melanie eyed him suspiciously, although she had to admit she had felt some butterflies in her stomach when he had winked at her. Tim then began to help her finish with the milk order and then he headed somewhere leaving Melanie to fend for herself the whole morning. Luckily, she was only scheduled to be the manager in charge until 10 a.m.

"Yo," Tim called to Melanie, sticking his head between the two large flappy doors that led to the back. He held his arm out like he was handing her something. As she got closer, she saw the manager keys in his hands. "Hold on to these for me, okay?"

Melanie was hesitant to take them. "But technically I'm not the manager in charge anymore today. I can get in trouble for holding those."

"It's fine," Tim said carelessly. "Just don't flaunt them if Raylayna comes around."

Melanie took them reluctantly, working the rest of her day with her head over her shoulder looking for any sight of Raylana. A few hours later, one of the other managers named Azalea came in for the closing shift. Melanie couldn't wait to get the keys out of her hands. As she and Melanie went into the office to do the shift turnover protocols, they talked about Tim.

"I can't believe Paulina is out," Azalea sighed as she counted the safe. "What's this guy's story?" she asked, referring to Tim.

"He seems average," Melanie said. "He barely even talked to me or helped me the whole day and then he made me hold the keys while he headed off to who knows where. I bet I could do a better job than him and the new district manager seems like a real bitch.

Right on cue, the office door opened and in walked Tim, carrying a piece of white computer paper. He glanced in their direction and then went straight for Azalea. "Here," he said without an introduction, handing her the paper. "I need all of this done before you go home."

Azalea took the paper and shot a side-glance to Melanie that said, *I see what you mean.*

"Well, I'm out of here. I had a long first day." said Melanie.

As Melanie walked towards the door, Tim stopped her. "Wait," he said. "Let's exchange numbers in case we need to get in touch."

For a second, Melanie thought about giving him a fake number, although she knew that would do no good because he could just look her up in the computer. *God, what am I thinking? He's just a coworker. Nothing is going to come out of him having my number.* "Alright," she said. "Let me see your phone, I'll punch mine in."

"No way," Tim said defensively. "I'll give you my number. Then you can just text me saying 'It's me.'"

Melanie thought it was weird that Tim wouldn't let her touch his phone but was too tired to argue. Fishing her phone out of her pocket, she opened up the keypad and said, "Go ahead." After she had put his number into her phone he immediately said "Give me your number now as well... just in case." Melanie quickly gave him her number then headed out to her car and drove home.

Later that night, around 11 p.m., Melanie was fresh out of the shower and ready to fall face-first into bed. Her first day had been a long one. No sooner did she turn out her bedroom light and get into bed when her text message alert went off. Sighing, she kicked her blanket off, got out of bed, and walked across the room to her phone. It was a text message from Tim.

Tim: Who is Amanda?

He must be reading an old schedule, Melanie realized.

Melanie: She quit.

Clicking her power button, she put her phone back on the charger and returned to bed. A few seconds later, her text message alert went off again. Trying to ignore it, she turned on her side and pulled her blanket over her head. Five minutes passed and she was just about to fall asleep when she heard it again.

Tim: U work tomorrow?

Tim: Don't ignore me.

Melanie got up again and opened the messaging application.

Melanie: You know I have to open tomorrow.

Tim: Lol. I know. ☺

Chapter 4: Thrown Under the Bus

The next morning, Melanie walked into the office to find a note left on the computer desk and couldn't help but roll her eyes when she read it.

Melanie – Be sure to throw out all the leftover Halloween merchandise today. It has to be gone before inventory. Have Azalea help you when she gets there; it's a lot. I tried some of the candy last night. It's sweet like you. P.S. throw this note out before Raylayna sees it.

The morning ran like it was her first time again: she struggled to build a fresh, pretty produce display, Raylayna showed up before the store opened, dug through the produce display and wrecked it, and then yelled at Melanie for missing some rotten grapes. A few hours later, Azalea showed up and they began to put out the old Halloween merchandise together.

"Tim told me that he tried some of this candy last night and that it was 'sweet like me,'" Melanie said.

Azalea grimaced. "Ew. What a weirdo."

Melanie smiles. "Yeah, he's crazy if he thinks he can get with me. I already have a boyfriend and I have to focus on my work goals or I'll never get promoted again. I've already gotten this far."

"Plus you know managers aren't allowed to date each other," Azalea pointed out as she propped open the back door.

"Are we supposed to write this stuff down?" Melanie asked as they started to chuck old candy and decorations into the dumpster.

"I'm not sure," Azalea said. "We usually write down all the Christmas stuff that we throw away. Why don't you ask Tim?"

"I think we had better write it down just in case," Melanie said, grabbing the clipboard off the wall. "When Paulina comes back, I want to make sure that everything is in order. I want her to be able to see that I can run the store when she's away much better than anyone else."

"Good idea," Azalea agreed. "Maybe we should call Paulina and ask her."

"Nah," Melanie said. "I don't want to bother her while she's trying to recover. I'm pretty sure we're good as long as we write it all down."

There was so much Halloween merchandise to throw away that it took Melanie and Azalea an hour to go through everything. The next day, to Melanie's relief, Tim and Raylayna were busy all morning doing inventory. Melanie and Azalea both ran the shift and nobody bothered them. It was great. As Melanie was fixing up the display by the entrance, Azalea came jogging over.

"Raylayna wants to see us in the office."

"Now what?" asked Melanie slightly exasperated.

Melanie and Azalea walked into the office cautiously. Tim and Raylayna were both sitting in front of the computer. As soon as the door shut behind them, Raylayna swiveled around in her chair and looked at both of them intensely.

"Who entered the discarded Halloween merchandise into the computer?" she snapped without hesitation.

Melanie and Azalea exchanged confused glances.

"Well we both wrote it down," Melanie said.

"That's nice," Raylayna said nastily. "But nobody claimed it. And now we have a $1,500 loss."

"Nobody told us," Melanie shrugged helplessly, shooting a meaningful glance at Tim.

Raylayna breathed out of her nose. "Luckily, we can fix it," she scoffed, "but it's a pain, and it doesn't make us look good at headquarters."

Later that afternoon, Melanie stood in the back doorway and watched Tim casually eating a chocolate donut. Puffing her chest, she walked toward him, ready to confront.

"What was that all about in the office?" she demanded.

"What was all what about?" he shrugged, feigning innocence.

"There was nothing in that note about actually entering the Halloween merchandise into the computer. All I got was that comment about how sweet I am. How was I supposed to know? *You're* the salary management trainee," Melanie barked. "*You* should have gotten in trouble for not entering the candy."

"You are sweet," Tim said, leaning on the broom, "and you're sexy when you're mad."

Melanie threw her hands in the air. "Ugh! For your information, I have a boyfriend. And I have goals. None of which include getting with my temporary boss."

"Temporary?" Tim repeated. "Don't count on it. I'm trying to get this store for myself. Then you'll be stuck with me forever."

"Then I'll put in for a transfer," Melanie replied sarcastically.

"Hey, listen," Tim said, reaching into his back pocket and taking out his wallet. He pulled out a 20-dollar bill. "I was up all last night and I'm exhausted. I'll give you 20 dollars to unload everything in the freezer today."

"Why are you so lazy?"

"Why are you so tense?"

"I'm not tense! You suck at your job. You don't even want to do it. Now you're paying me cash. For your information, you can't buy me."

Tim smiled arrogantly. "You can buy almost anything."

Chapter 5: Super Bowl Sunday

A few months later, Melanie was doing alright for herself. It took longer than she thought possible to adjust to Tim's easy going management style and Raylayna's wrathful nature, but she was starting to come into her own as an Assistant Manager, even though they might as well have called her the manager. Although her openings weren't the best, her closings were great, so Tim often scheduled her for nights. Tim was of little to no help teaching her anything new so Melanie secretly called Paulina once a week to get her advice on things until she really got into the groove.

It was a Saturday night, the day before Super Bowl Sunday, and the store was packed. Tim and Melanie stood in the office doing the safe turnover. Tim was relentless with his compliments and crude come on attempts to Melanie, but luckily for her, she'd learned how to tune it out and deal with him, although she did occasionally have crazy dreams about him at night that left her horny and agitated in the mornings. She had trouble ignoring his cute dimples and wondered if she could change him... make him more of a gentleman.

Just when she had finished an inventory count Tim walked up and said: "You've gotten so much better since I first got here," as he flashed a genuine smile at her.

"Don't flatter me," Meanie replied, although she did appreciate the compliment after all this time.

"No, really," Tim said. "I'm glad you're my assistant."

"I'm not assisting you with anything. If anything, I cover your ass and make your job easier."

"Would you rather I called you my side chick?"

Melanie was usually calm when he made his little jokes... but she was tempted to threaten him with all the inside information she had him. She quickly changed her mind when she could sense that he was genuinely trying to be humorous and not hurtful. "I have to get to work," Melanie said, turning away while hitting him in the face with her long brown hair.

"Listen," Tim said. "I've got to do inventory of our perishables tomorrow morning. We can't count any of the new stuff, so don't put any new meat or bread out. I also have to count what produce is already out on the floor, so don't even bother filling it tonight. Let it run down to nothing."

"Are you sure?" Melanie frowned. "If Raylayna comes in and sees that, she'll freak out."

"No, no, no, it's fine," Tim insisted confidently. "She's not coming around today. And I'll take the blame if she does." He winked. "Our secret."

"If you say so," Melanie said doubtfully.

A few hours later, Melanie was standing in aisle 2, cleaning up the store and ignoring the perishables like Tim told her too. Suddenly, she heard an icy voice that made chills form down her spine.

"Hey Melanie, how's it going tonight?"

Melanie froze in place and turned her neck to see Raylayna standing there with her arms crossed. She did not look happy.

"It's going good," Melanie uttered.

Raylayna raised an eyebrow. "Oh yeah? So then why is the produce display half empty?"

"Because of the perishable inventory," Melanie said confidently.

Raylayna's face turned dark red. "I don't care about the perishable inventory!" she erupted, punching her fist into her palm. "We've had countless meetings about the importance of keeping the produce display filled at all times!" She flung her arm out to span the store. "Look at how many sales we're missing out on! Why? Why wouldn't you fill it?"

Melanie took a step back, eyes wide. She was trapped between Raylayna and the shelves. "Because Tim has to count it tomorrow," she insisted.

"I don't give a damn about the perishable inventory," Raylayna angrily repeated, her accent in full throttle. "I've counted *plenty* without letting the display run down!" Her rant was far from over. "I cannot tell you how disappointed I am. We've been over this time after time. No wonder this store is out of control."

Inside, Melanie's adrenaline was pumping. She felt cornered, trapped. Her face burned hot and she wanted to fall off the face of the Earth, never to return. All of the shoppers in the store stopped and turned to look at the scene Raylayna was making.

"Tim told me to let it run down!" she finally blurted out, trying to stop her tears from flowing .

Raylayna backed up and thought for a moment. "Why would Tim tell you to do that?" she asked in a much calmer voice. It was almost too calm. "I'll follow up with him on that."

With that, Raylayna blew out of the store. Melanie could finally breathe a sigh of relief and continued to clean. A few minutes later, her phone went off. It was a group text message from Tim, copied to the other managers in the store.

Tim: Manager meeting tomorrow: 5:30 a.m.

Chapter 6: Last Chance

The manager meeting was early and rough. Raylayna basically repeated what she said to Melanie the night before, though with a much calmer demeanor. After the meeting, Raylayna pulled Melanie to the side.

"Melanie, last night you told me that Tim told you to let the produce display run down," she said. "I spoke with Tim and he said that he does not recall saying anything like that to you before he left."

Melanie's blood ran cold. *"That motherfucker!!"* she thought.

"Maybe I just misheard him," Melanie shrugged, throwing out the first lie she could come up with. She wasn't trying to argue with Raylayna today.

"I know you want to be a salary store manager," Raylayna continued. "You know that this company prides itself on honesty. I am shocked that you would lie to me, Melanie. It makes me wonder if you're really serious about this job. I am forced to put you on probation. This is your last chance. If I find out you've lied or gone against our store policy again, I will have no choice but to let you go." With that, she turned on her heels and left.

Melanie bit a mouthful of words for Tim all day but, conveniently, he never seemed to be in the same department she was. Out of the corner of her eye, she saw him walk in the back room and stealthily followed. Hiding behind a pallet of water bottles, she watched him enter the freezer. *Gotcha!*

As soon as Tim disappeared behind the flaps in the doorway, Melanie ran to follow him, closing the door behind them.

Melanie pointed at him. She felt all of her blood rush to her fingertip. "You!"

Tim just looked at her in silence though his eyes screamed "guilty."

"You threw me under the bus!"

He finally spoke. "What do you mean?"

Melanie rolled her eyes. "I don't recall."

Tim threw his hands up. "Alright, alright, my fault," he admitted reluctantly. "You know Raylayna is scary and this is my one shot at proving I can run a store. I didn't want to get in trouble."

"So you got *me* in trouble?" Melanie exclaimed, shaking her head. "Do you know what she said to me? Do you know?"

"No what?"

"She told me that if I lie or break any of the company rules again, she'll fire me."

Tim smiled and laughed under his breath. Melanie seriously thought that she had what it took to punch him in the face.

"It's not funny!"

"Relax, side chick," he said without concern. "She's all bark and no bite."

"So then why were you afraid to come clean to her and decided to use me as a target?" Melanie interrogated. "And don't call me that. I'm not your side chick."

Tim cocked his head. "You could be if you wanted to. You should feel special because I'm engaged."

Melanie felt a sinking feeling in her heart. *Ugh, here we go again.*

"Don't make me throw up," Melanie opened the door and turned to leave. "Besides, you're my boss. My *temporary* boss. You're not worth my job."

Tim's face shifted into something like hurt. "Ouch."

The next morning, Melanie had to come in for the midshift, but she overslept, plagued by dreams of work that sapped her strength and had her waking up in a panic feeling exhausted. She quickly threw her clothes on and ran out the door, racing down the highway to Save 'n Bag. Running into the office, she stopped short when she saw Tim sitting at the lunch table, lounging about like there was nothing to do.

"Good morning, sunshine," Tim teased as she went to punch in.

"I'm not talking to you," Melanie announced as she reached into her pants pocket to grab her phone. "How many minutes late am I really?"

A look of panic suddenly painted her face. She vigorously patted the sides of her pants, hoping to feel the bulge of her phone, but it wasn't there. Grabbing her bag, she ripped it open and searched relentlessly.

"My phone!" she exclaimed. "I think I left my phone at home!"

Tim smirked. "That sucks."

"No, you don't understand," Melanie sputtered. "I have things on there that my boyfriend can't see and he's home."

Tim's eyes lit up. "Things your boyfriend can't see, huh? So the tables are turning and I do have a chance?"

Melanie rolled her eyes and absentmindedly admitted, "I guess you can say I'm somewhat of an attention whore." She glanced wildly, her eyes to the clock on the wall. "You *gotta* let me go get it. Change my schedule in the computer so I'm not late." Then she said something that she never thought she'd say in a million years. "It'll be our secret"

"Alright," Tim shrugged, smiling because he knew he had her in a vulnerable position. "But you better hurry. I heard Raylayna is lurking in the area."

"I owe you!" was all Melanie could manage to say before she bolted out the door. Jumping into her car, she raced down the highway until she finally made it to her house. As she opened the car door to step out, she heard a loud thud drop onto the ground. Bending down, she picked up her phone off the asphalt, feeling stupid that it was in her car the entire time.

A half hour later, she returned to work and was stocking the cooler when Tim slid through the door with a couple of boxes.

"Hey," he mumbled in a low voice as Melanie loaded up a shelf with cases of potato salad. "I just wanted to say that you're awesome for what happened before."

"What happened before?"

"You having to go get your phone because it had dirty things on it that your boyfriend doesn't know about," Tim said, his eyes glowing. "I knew you had it in you. I guess you could say that I'm kind of an attention whore myself."

That explains why he wouldn't let me touch his phone when I met him. Melanie shot him a disapproving look. "Aren't you engaged?"

"Yes," Tim replied, moving closer. "But I'm not married *yet*. I've been with the same girl for seven years and I'm about to be stuck with her for the rest of my life. You can't blame a guy for wanting to get in as much fun as he can before he signs it all away."

"Are you implying what I think you are?"

"It can be our secret," Tim smiled.

Melanie maintained a sarcastic expression on her face but felt a warm twinge inside of her pants. She hated Tim but, at the same time, she'd wanted him since the moment she saw him. This whole time she denied it because she had already been seeing someone else, but now that she was completely sure of his intentions, she had to admit, it was tempting.

"And how much longer will this window of opportunity be open?" she said sarcastically, flashing him one of his own arrogant smiles.

Tim put his arms on her waist and started to rub his hips against her. "Right now, it's only open for you, baby."

Melanie opened her mouth to say something but before she could, the moment was ruined by the sound of Raylayna rushing through the flaps of the cooler door, startling them both. They quickly jumped away from each other and tried to act innocent.

"Why are we all just standing around?" Raylayna demanded, oblivious to what she had just interrupted. She threw up her wrist and looked at her watch. "It's already one o'clock and all these perishables have been sitting out since eight. We need to get them back into the cooler right away."

"We were just finishing up the cooler."

"Well hurry up. The losses in this store are at an all-time high. We can't afford to lose any more inventory," she snarled before turning around and walking out of the back room. As soon as she was gone, Tim and Melanie looked at each other, relieved.

"That was close," Tim chuckled.

"Yeah," Melanie nodded, holding her chest with her hand. "If we do this, we'll have to be extra careful."

"Why?"

"Because you're my boss – my temporary boss, I mean - and Raylayna said I have one more chance. What if we just waited until you left the store?"

"Who knows when that could be," Tim said. "I could be married by then, and then I'll feel obligated to not do anything."

Melanie's heart was pounding and this excitement was turning her on, but in the back of her head, she remembered how hard she had worked to get where she was and she didn't want to risk it all for one night of pleasure. "What about you? Aren't you afraid of losing your job?"

"I'm not afraid of anything," Tim said proudly.

Melanie couldn't help but laugh. "Not even Raylayna?"

"Maybe a little," Tim smiled, showing those cute dimples again.

Shaking her head, trying not to laugh herself, Melanie walked out of the cooler, swaying her hips a bit. Just outside the cooler was Azalea.

"What are you smiling about?" she asked.

"Oh nothing," Melanie said, hurrying away.

Chapter 7: Feeling Empty

About a week later, Melanie was on vacation and she couldn't have been happier to be away from it all – Tim, the grocery store, Raylayna, and most of all, the conflict of possibly wanting to jump on her boss – her temporary boss, as she liked to refer to him.

She relaxed on the couch, watching TV. Her boyfriend was lying on the couch next to her but he wasn't paying much attention to her. He hadn't been giving her much attention or support for the last several months.

"So, what do you want to do today?" Melanie asked him.

"I don't care," her boyfriend shrugged. "You pick."

"I can't believe this. You've known that I was going on vacation for months now and you couldn't even plan anything nice for me?" Melanie complained. "What, you just want me to spend my vacation taking care of all your needs and whims?" Melanie said, getting more heated.

"I'm just so bored," her boyfriend complained.

"Ugggh… He is such a downer" she thought.

She began to ignore him. Suddenly, she felt her phone vibrate.

Tim: I miss you so much.

Melanie cracked a little smile and felt butterflies in her stomach. It felt so good to be desired. Her boyfriend barely paid attention to her at all when she was home. She immediately got up and went to the bathroom for some privacy.

Melanie: I miss you too. Having a hard time running the store without me?

Tim: Seriously. Raylayna has been on a warpath all week. She yelled at me this morning. I was kind of hoping she gave me an ultimatum too, because now I'd risk my job for you.

Melanie: What would your fiancé say when you lose your job?

Tim: No worries, I'll just lie. You should send me a picture of you. I miss your sexy face.

Melanie surfed through her pictures, looking for one suitable to send Tim. Most of them were pretty bad selfies. Finally, she stumbled upon a nice one that her friend had taken of her on the beach.

Tim: Send me another one...a sexier one ☺

Melanie: Hell no. What if you lose your phone at work?

Tim: Take one without your face in the picture.

Melanie: It will still show under my name.

Tim: I'll delete the message thread from you after I download it.

Melanie stared into space. The truth was, she didn't have any of those kinds of pictures on her phone. She never felt comfortable taking them, but she had never admitted that to her boyfriend. Somehow, Tim's interest made her feel confident lately.

Slipping into the bathroom, she undressed herself and started the shower. Stepping inside, she pulled back the curtain and tilted her hair under the hot water. Grabbing the shampoo bottle, she gently massages her fingertips into the top of her sexy long hair. Then, she grabs some shower gel and pours it over her smooth, silky skin, rubbing it in with a brand new luxurious white sponge. As she rubs the gel onto her chest, her breasts bounce up and down as she gets a thick lather of bubbles going. Suddenly, the bathroom door opens and the shower curtain is pulled back, revealing her boyfriend's head smiling at her eagerly.

"Hey, sexy," he says as he climbs in and starts to massage her large lathered up breasts softly with his hands. After a minute of this Melanie sighs and makes room for him in the shower and then proceeds to bend over while rubbing his balls from underneath. It was both of their favorite position. All they ever did any more was have sex. At least Tim was interested in getting to know her. As her boyfriend worked his manhood into her and began to thrust back and forth, she closed her eyes and pretended it was Tim when she climaxed powerfully.

Chapter 8: A Picture is Worth 1,000 Words

As soon as her boyfriend finished and slipped back out of the shower, Melanie dried herself off and grabbed her phone off of the bathroom sink. Dropping the towel from around her naked body, she opened up the camera and started to take pictures. The first few were kind of blurry. She stretched herself out in front of the mirror above the sink, held her two breasts up with her hands, and snapped a few more. Finally, she held the camera above her and took a nice, clear shot. Even though she got part of her face in it, she decided that Tim would appreciate that one the most and sent it.

A few minutes later, her text message notification went off again and she bit her lip in anticipation.

Tim: Did you take the picture yet?

Melanie frowned in confusion.

Melanie: Yeah, I just sent it. Didn't you get it?

Tim: No I didn't get anything.

Melanie's eyes bulged. *Oh no, who did I send it to then?* Opening the overview of her text messages, her heart sank when she saw the first name at the top of her list: Raylayna. *No! No, no, no!*

"Shit!" Melanie whispered out loud to herself.

"What?" her boyfriend, who was sitting nearby again, asked?

Melanie turned her back. "Nothing, just work stuff."

She waited for her phone to ring with Raylayna on the other line, giddy that she got to use the "We have to let you go" speech. Hours passed and she got nothing, not even a reply text message. She thought about calling Azalea or even Paulina, but how could she tell them what kind of situation she was in? Shooting a glance to her fridge, she looked at when she was due to work again – tomorrow morning. Feeling sick to her stomach, she threw her phone to the side and laid down in her bed...tomorrow, she would lose it all.

Chapter 9: The End

"What's your problem?" Tim greeted Melanie as she walked into the office, fell against the wall and slid down to the floor.

"I know who got that picture I was supposed to send you," she replied.

"Who?"

Melanie's cheeks turned red. "Raylayna."

Tim threw his head back and burst out laughing.

Melanie glared at him. "I don't see what's so funny about this. I'm going to lose my job and now *you're* going to have to put in twice the work."

"Okay, okay, I'm sorry," Tim said emotionlessly as he wiped some tears from his eyes. "Damn, what a waste of a picture, though."

Behind them, the breakroom door opened and slammed shut, followed by a clicking sound with every footstep. Raylayna was there in her black high heels. She wasted no time in starting her rant. In her arms, she carried an assortment of items from the sliding freezers.

"*Who* put these items out last week?" she snapped, opening her arms and letting the items drop onto the floor with a loud thud. "None of them were stamped with a date. Now we have to throw all of these out. There is at least $500 worth of food here! If nobody owns up to this, we are having another meeting at five in the morning!"

Melanie looked at Tim. She knew he had to be the one who put those items out without a date.

"I'm waiting," Raylayna interrupted as she stood with her arms crossed and tapped her foot. "I'm tired of all the losses in this store. Things are about to change *very* soon."

Just as she saw Tim open his mouth to say something, Melanie blurted out, "It was me!"

Tim and Raylyna both looked at her. Melanie knew she was in trouble as it was. She might as well do something for Tim to rack up some points. Once she was fired, it was game time.

"Wait, what?" Tim exclaimed.

"It was me. I put them out like that."

"Good, I want to talk to you anyway," Raylayna snarled. "Tim, may we have a minute alone?"

Tim's eyes bulged out at Melanie as if to say, *What the hell are you doing?* A few moments later, he stepped out. Melanie picked herself up off the floor, looked at Raylayna, and gulped.

Chapter 10: An Act of Kindness

Later that day, Melanie lay in bed with all the lights out and the blanket over her head. She wanted nothing to do with the outside world. Everything she had ever worked for vanished right in front of her eyes that morning. She hadn't even called Paulina yet. How the hell was she supposed to explain *that*?

Struggling to hold back tears, her heart suddenly jolted when her cell phone began to ring. Trying not to get her hopes up, she picked it up and looked at the screen. It was Tim.

"Hello?" she croaked into the phone, trying to clear the phlegm from her throat.

"Hello Mrs. Melanie," she heard on the other line. "Don't sound so happy to hear from me."

"Are you serious right now? Do you know what I feel like?"

"I'm about to make you feel better, babe."

"Now isn't the time for you to play Mr. Suave," Melanie shot back.

"No, no, no," Tim said. "I'm calling with good news."

"What kind of news?"

"I got you your job back."

Melanie instantly shot up. The blankets went flying off her head. She quickly moved her hand to turn on the lights. "What?"

"I told Raylayna what happened. I told her it was my fault. The picture *and* the undated items."

"Oh my god," Melanie gasped. "You sold yourself out? *You* sold *yourself* out to Raylayna?"

"It was the least I could do. You know I have a big ego, but in the last few months we worked together, I have to admit that if you weren't there, I don't think I could have run the store by myself. I know how hard you've been working and I didn't think you deserved what happened. I play around a lot, but it's hard for me to admit stuff like that," Tim confessed. "I know I can be a dick, but I can be a nice guy, too. I just didn't think a girl as pretty and as hardworking as you deserved what happened."

Melanie felt more tears in her eyes, but this time, they were happy tears. Her heart swelled in her chest. Then she suddenly snapped back to reality. "So what do I owe you now? Do I have to suck your dick for this?"

"Let's just call this one a free pass. I've done a lot of douchebag things in my life but nobody has ever taken the hit for me. That was really cool, Mel. Really cool."

Melanie pouted her lips. "So I guess you're leaving me now, huh?"

"Nope, you're still stuck with me!"

"What? Damn!" Melanie frowned. So close. "How did you bypass Raylayna on this one?"

Tim chuckled arrogantly. "Let's just say she thinks I'm hot, too."

Shaking her head, Melanie laughed.

Chapter 11: Another Opportunity

Melanie proudly walked into work the next morning. Looking around at her surroundings, she smiled and realized just how grateful she was for her job. Tim greeted her as she walked into the office.

"Have you heard the news? I'm leaving you next week. Your girl Paulina is coming back."

"Hold on, let me fall to the ground crying," Melanie joked. Then she smiled. "But seriously, we've been through a lot in the past 6 months. When I first met you, I thought you were a douchebag. I had no intention of talking to you, but I'm glad we met. Don't forget me when you get your own store."

Tim smiled, but this time it wasn't sarcastic or funny. His smile was genuine and his eyes crinkled up as his gaze swept Melanie's toned body. "I could never forget you."

Melanie stuck her tongue out at him in response.

"It's not funny, I'm serious," he insisted.

"Prove it."

"Since I'm not technically your boss anymore, come over to my apartment tonight. My fiancé won't be home. She's going out with the girls for her bachelorette party."

Melanie crossed her arms. "You want me to drive an hour away to your house when I have to open tomorrow?"

"It will be worth it," Tim assured her. Then, flashing his trademark dimpled smile, he winked and added, "And since I'm here for another 6 days, it will be our secret."

Chapter 12: Last Chance

Fresh out of the shower, wearing her most revealing purple silk top and donning some light makeup, Melanie made the hour drive to Tim's house, hoping that it would be a decision that she wouldn't regret. As she pulled onto the dark street and slowed to a stop behind Tim's parked car, she paused for a minute and thought about what she was doing. Was it really the right thing to do? Like Paulina always said, Melanie could do anything she put her mind to.

She thought about how hard she worked prior to Paulina's injury to get where she was now. She thought about how she survived Raylayna's reign, but she also thought about how seriously she always took everything. Melanie was a workaholic. She barely ever rewarded or even made time for herself. Now was her opportunity, and she wasn't about to let it go. If her boyfriend didn't appreciate her she was curious to see if Tim could back up all of his talk and pay her back for all the trouble he had caused her.

Turning the car off, she opened the door and stepped outside. Her hair blew gently in the low breeze that wafted through the air.

"Wow, you look beautiful."

Melanie jumped at the sudden sound of Tim's voice, the way she did when he rang the store doorbell on his first day. Turning, she saw him lingering on his front porch dressed in nothing but a pair of silky black boxers. Melanie's muscular imagination of him when they first met was also right. His chest was broad and muscular and he had very nice shoulders.

Melanie blushed. "Thank you."

Tim smiled as he leaned over the railing on the porch. "Come on in off the street, babe," he said, reaching out his arm. "You're no good to me all the way over there."

As Melanie made her way to his front door, her stomach flip-flopped. She couldn't believe what she was about to do. He was confident, as always, which set her at ease.

Tim went to take her jacket off as soon as the door closed behind them. "Take your coat off," he said. "Stay a while."

Grabbing her hand, he quickly led her into the bedroom, like a child waiting to open presents on Christmas morning.

Melanie grabbed onto the side of the doorway. "Wait!"

Tim immediately turned around. "What?"

"What if your fiancé comes home early?"

"Don't worry," Tim laughed confidently, swooping his arms around her, picking her up, and throwing her over his shoulder. "She's staying out overnight."

"Hey, let me down!" Melanie said playfully.

"I got you now, babe," Tim replied as they disappeared into the bedroom. "I'd never put you down now."

Chapter 13: Our Secret

As soon as they were through the door, they wasted no time. Tim threw her down onto the bed and pounced on top of her.

"I've been waiting for this moment since I first saw you," he whispered.

Melanie wore a sleeveless leopard-print shirt with a zipper down the middle that hugged her body. Tim grabbed the the zipper and slowly pulled it down. As it lowered, he licked Melanie's neck as her large breasts slowly popped out one at a time. He instantly got hard when he saw she was wearing no bra underneath. Tim cupped them both in his large hands, playing with each nipple, squeezing, licking, and sucking on them. Melanie loved it! She had been secretly dreaming of this. It was finally here and it was living up to her expectations!

As Tim nibbled on each nipple with his teeth, Melanie cupped her arms around his naked back and dug her fingertips into him, arching her back with every flick of his tongue. As her waist rose, Tim slid his hands down her body, sending chills up her spine. He grabbed her waist, holding her still. Pulling himself up into place, he started to rub himself against her until a large bulge pressed through his boxers.

When Melanie felt his hardness, she also felt herself get warm and wet underneath. Lying back, she let Tim tease her with is hard cock enjoying every second of it. Tim then slowly pulled off her pants, licking her legs the whole way down. He then licked his way up again, as he gently pulled off her panties. "Ahhh," he moans in ecstasy as he entered her slowly while Melanie groans in both pain and pleasure as he is much larger than her husband.

"Tell me you want me," Tim gasps as he starts to push his way in further. "Tell me how bad you want me."

Melanie squeezed her eyes shut, threw her head back and screamed, "I want you, Tim. I want you so bad."

Tim begin to thrust even harder then, entering her fully. Melanie was in ecstasy and she was cumming hard after just a few minutes of this. Tim then repositioned himself, pushed her legs apart and started to use his tongue to get every last bit of ecstasy she had left in her. As he slowly ran his silky, warm tongue against her pussy, he looked up at her.

"Oh yes," Melanie whispered. "Yes!" she said with pure joy in her eyes.

He smiled at her... crouched and at full attention. "I've been wanting to do this forever." He stated in a sultry voice as he bent her over his bed and entered her from behind while grabbing all her hair up in one big fist. It felt so good to him and it wasn't much longer before he had pulled out and creamed all over her butt, back and the ends of her long brown hair.

After that they had a nice glass of wine. But it wasn't long before Tim was kissing Melanie passionately in the kitchen, both of their tongues exploring.

Tim lifted her onto the kitchen counter and licked her passionately between her legs until he knew that she was about to cum again in the heat of the moment. He then stopped and started put his hard cock inside her again.

Just as he started to press it inside, Melanie tensed. Using his large hands, he kneaded her neck. "Relax babe," he said. "You're about the have the fuck of a lifetime. I am always better the second time around."

Gently pressing against her, he eases in and starts to move in and out slowly, moaning with the pure pleasure of feeling as Melanie's body is wrapped around his length. Gradually, he starts to thrust faster and faster until Melanie's body is rocking back and forth so hard that she has to put her hands on the counter to keep her balance. .

"Yeah!" Tim shouted as he fucked her. "Give it to me, baby! Give me all of this pussy!"

Melanie moaned in reply.

"I'm about to cum, babe," Tim gasped in desperation. "You want me to cum in you?"

"Yes," Melanie uttered as she was about to climax herself.

Tim grabs her hair and pulls her beautiful face towards his. "Yes what?"

"Yes sir," Melanie replied as she began to have one of the best orgasms of her life.

Tim could only moan in reply as he began to thrust powerfully into her, his girth expanding with each of his orgasmic spasms. Tilting his head back, he began to pound even harder, his breathe heavy and the moans he produced where loud and deep. Tim had never known as much joy in his life as he was experiencing now. It was pure heaven and he felt like king of the world.

Both of them gasped for air, their movement slowly coming to a halt as Tim released himself from inside of her.

"Ahh," Tim sighed, releasing his grip. Melanie let her body fall into the pillows. "Damn babe, that was amazing," he said as he lay next to her. Looking into her eyes, he playfully pushed her lovely brown hair out of her face.

"That was great," Melanie agreed.

They both lay there for a while, enjoying what had just happened and taking comfort in their embrace. Then Melanie said wistfully "It's too bad that you're getting married soon."

"Yeah," Tim said sadly. Then a smile crept onto his face. "But you know what they say about cheaters. Once a cheater, always a cheater. Now that we've finally done it, I can feel less and less bad about it once I'm married."

"So you're saying you want to have an affair with me and you're not even married *yet*?"

"Sure, why not? We'll never know what it will lead to if we don't try."

Melanie grinned. "So let me guess...this will be our secret?"

Tim reached out and pulled Melanie into him, cuddling with her as she put her head on his chest. "You got that right, babe," he said. "If we do live happily ever after... this will all be our secret."

My Other Books and Audio Books

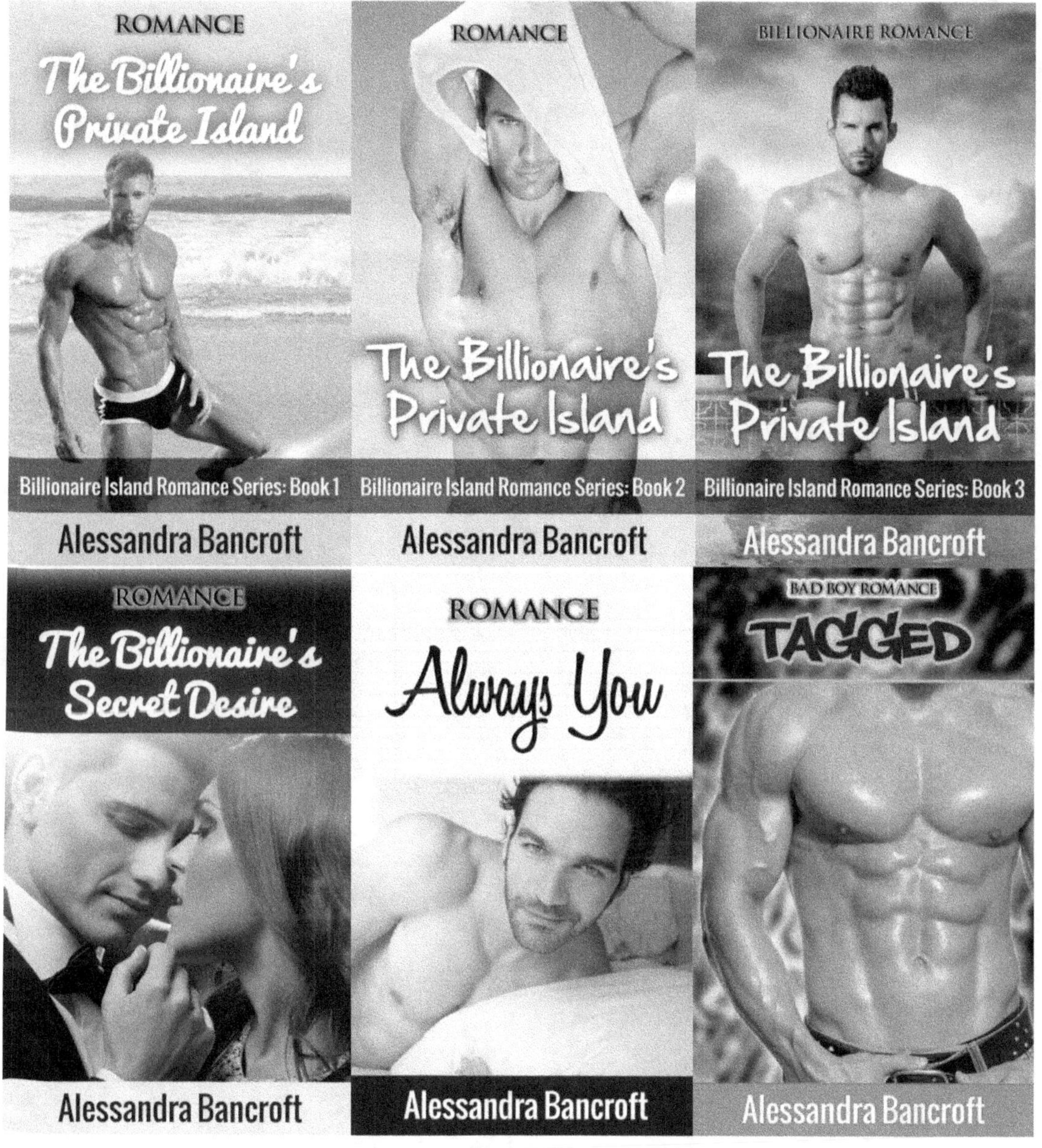

All of these are available in audio book as well.

If you enjoyed this book then please spare a few seconds to easily post a quick positive review. It would be greatly appreciated!

Thanks for reading.